First Grade Takes a Test

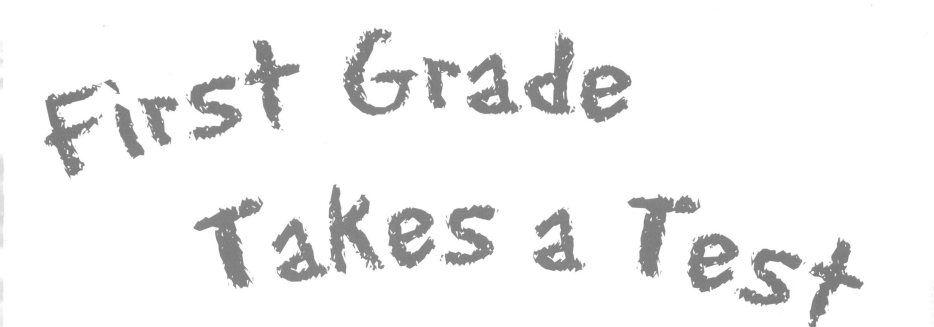

By Miriam Cohen

Illustrated by Ronald Himler

Star Bright Books
New York

Published in the United States of America by Star Bright Books, Inc., New York.
The name Star Bright Books and the Star Bright Books logo are registered
trademarks of Star Bright Books, Inc. Please visit www.starbrightbooks.com.

Hardback ISBN-13: 978-1-59572-054-2
Paperback ISBN-13: 978-1-59572-055-9

Previously published under ISBN 0-440-41093-2

Printed in Singapore (KHL) 9 8 7 6 5 4 3 2

Library of Congress Cataloging-in-Publication Data is available.

For Monroe who gave me the idea, and
for David who has lots of good ideas —M.C.

For Quinn Carter Smith —R.H.

With thanks to the North Dakota Study Group
on Evaluation—especially to Lillian Weber,
Deborah Meier, Ann Cook, and Vito Perrone

A lady from the principal's office
came to the first grade.
She had a big pile of papers
with little boxes all over them.

She smiled at the first grade.
"We have some tests for you," she said.
"Oh, good," said Anna Maria.
"Now we can find out how smart we are."

Their teacher told the first grade how to do the test. She said, "Read the questions carefully. Then take your pencil and fill in the box next to the right answer.

You must work quickly.
But do not worry—
you can do it.
Ready? Begin!"

George looked at the test. It said:

Rabbits eat:

☐ lettuce

☐ dog food

☐ sandwiches

He raised his hand.

"Rabbits have to eat carrots, or their teeth will get too long and stick into them," he said.

The teacher nodded and smiled, but she put her finger to her lips. George carefully drew in a carrot so the test people would know.

Sammy read:

What do firemen do?

☐ make bread

☐ put out fires

☐ sing

He poked Willy. "Firemen get your head out when it's stuck," he said. "My uncle had his head stuck in a big pipe, and the firemen came and got it out."

But none of the boxes said that.

On the test there was a picture of Sally and Tom. Sally was giving Tom something. It looked like a bologna sandwich. Underneath it said:

☐ Sally is taller than Tom.

☐ Tom is taller than Sally.

Jim wondered what being tall
had to do with getting a bologna
sandwich. And was it really a
bologna sandwich? It might be
tomato. . . Jim took a long
time on that one.

Suddenly the teacher said,
"Time is up!"

"I'm not finished!" cried
everyone except Anna Maria.
But the teacher had to take
the tests away.

Anna Maria was smiling
and telling everyone,
"That was *easy*."

"Ooh," Sara said. "I *know* I did it wrong!"
"Don't worry," Jim said. "You're as smart as I am."

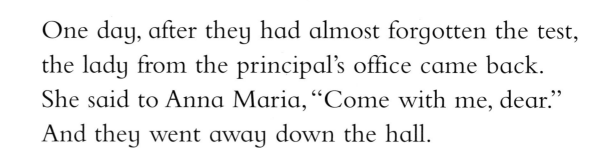

One day, after they had almost forgotten the test,
the lady from the principal's office came back.
She said to Anna Maria, "Come with me, dear."
And they went away down the hall.

When Margaret came back from getting a drink of water, she told everybody, "Anna Maria is in the special class because she did a good test!"

Everyone looked around the room.

Paul was mad. He said to Danny,
"*You're* not going with Anna Maria, dummy!"
"You're a dummy!" Danny said.
Everybody began calling someone else,
"Dummy! Dummy!"
Jim whispered to himself, "Dummy!"

"Listen to me!" the teacher said loudly.
The first grade class had never heard
their teacher sound like that.
"The test doesn't tell everything. It
doesn't tell all the things you *can* do!

You can build things! You can read books! You can make pictures! You have good ideas! And another thing. The test doesn't tell you if you are a kind person who helps your friends. Those are important things."

Everybody was quiet.
Then the teacher brought
out cookies she had made.

When Danny got his, he yelled,
"Sara got a fatter cookie than I did!"
"Mine is fatter, but yours is wider," Sara said.

"Let me see!" They all looked at Sara's and
Danny's cookies and felt them. But nobody
could tell which was bigger.

Jim said, "Let's weigh them!"
They rushed to the scale.

Both cookies weighed
the same!

"Good thinking,
Jim!" said the teacher.

Everybody went back to work.
Jim and Paul started fixing
their undersea racing car.
Sara sat in the rocker reading
a good book called *Worms:
Our Friends in the Earth*.

Margaret helped George
with his arithmetic.
By the time the bell rang,
everyone felt a lot better.

Every day, Anna Maria went to the special class. But first thing each morning, she peeked into the first grade to tell them things.

On Monday, she said, "Don't forget to water the plants."

On Tuesday, she asked, "Who is reminding the teacher when it is time to pass out the papers?"

On Wednesday, she told Sara, "Margaret doesn't know how to help George with his arithmetic."

On Thursday, she whispered something to the teacher.

And on Friday, when the first grade came running into their room, Anna Maria was sitting in the rocking chair.

"Aren't you in the special class anymore?" everyone asked.
"No," said Anna Maria. "I told them I had to come back.
I told them the first grade needs me."

"It's good to be together again," said the teacher. "We don't need a test to tell us that!"